PABLO AND SPLASH

SHEENA DEMPSEY

BLOOMSBURY
CHILDREN'S BOOKS

LONDON · OXFORD · NEW YORK · NEW DELHI · SYDNEY

PABLO

PROFESSOR O'BRAIN

1124

TEN

Books should be returned or renewed by the last date above. Renew by phone **03000 41 31 31** or online *www.kent.gov.uk/libs*

Libraries Registration & Archives

CUSTOMER SERVICE EXCELLENCE

CSE

Kent
County
Council
kent.gov.uk

For Mick

BLOOMSBURY CHILDREN'S BOOKS
Bloomsbury Publishing Plc
50 Bedford Square, London WC1B 3DP, UK
29 Earlsfort Terrace, Dublin 2, Ireland

BLOOMSBURY, BLOOMSBURY CHILDREN'S BOOKS and the Diana logo
are trademarks of Bloomsbury Publishing Plc

First published in Great Britain in 2024 by Bloomsbury Publishing Plc

A catalogue record for this book is available from the British Library

ISBN: PB: 978-1-5266-6260-6; eBook: 978-1-5266-6261-3; ePDF: 978-1-5266-6262-0

2 4 6 8 10 9 7 5 3 1

Printed and bound in China by C&C Offset Printing Co. Ltd, Shenzhen, Guangdong

To find out more about our authors and books
visit www.bloomsbury.com and sign up for our newsletters

SPLASH

PEBBLES BENJI PIPER

CHAPTER ONE

Antarctica. −58 ℃.

... a HOLIDAY.

A holiday?

No, not a holiday. A HOLIDAY. *Away* from Antarctica.

Where the sun has heat!

And the sea isn't frozen over.

Imagine warm sand between our toes instead of ice.

And tropical fish that taste like every colour of the southern lights.

4

Krill pops whenever we want?

And if they don't take our fancy, a krillwich?

Or scrambled krill?

Or — my chickhood favourite — regurgitated krill?

BLARGH!

8

9

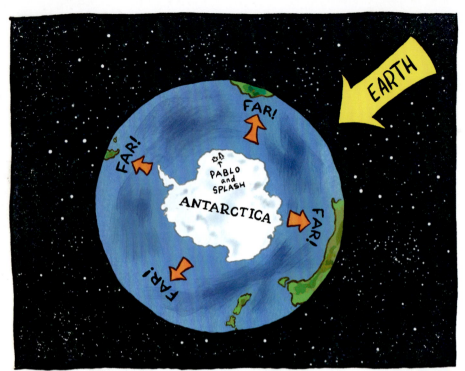

You're the brains here — I was hoping you'd figure out all the log ... the logish ... the logstickys ...

The logistics?

SNIFF ... yeah.

Ooo! It might be time for my favourite thing! A **LIST**!

PROS

1. FUN
2. WARM
3. DIFFERENT
4. EXCITING

CONS

1. HOW TO GET THERE?

CHAPTER TWO

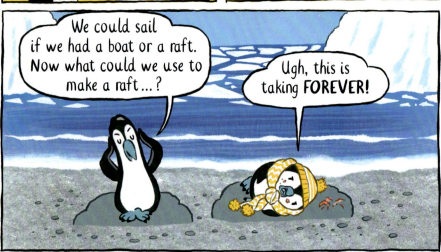

18

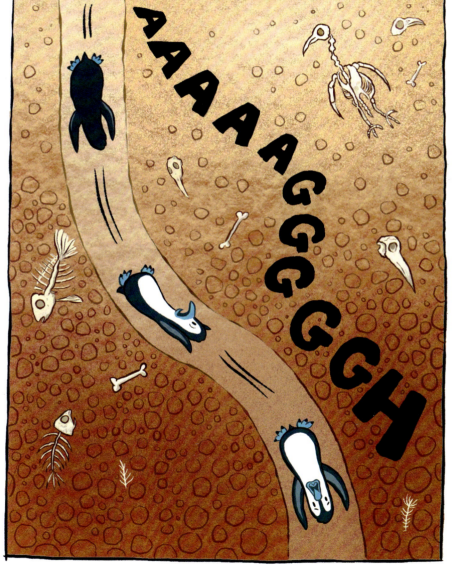

28

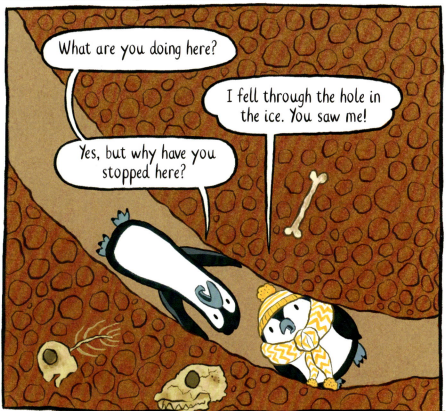

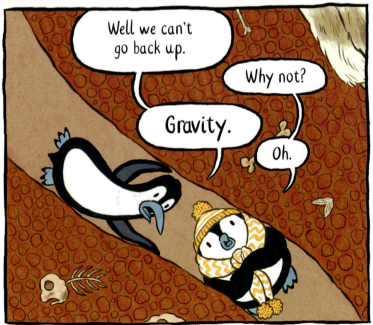

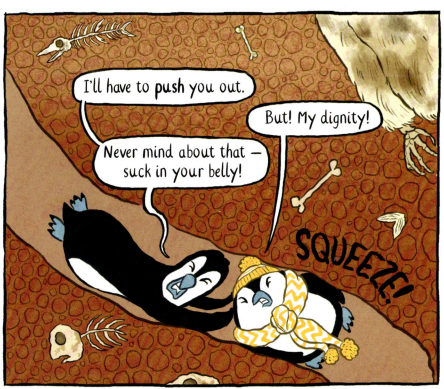

31

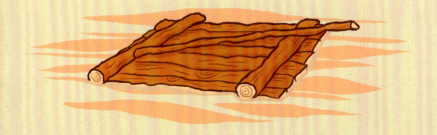

CHAPTER THREE

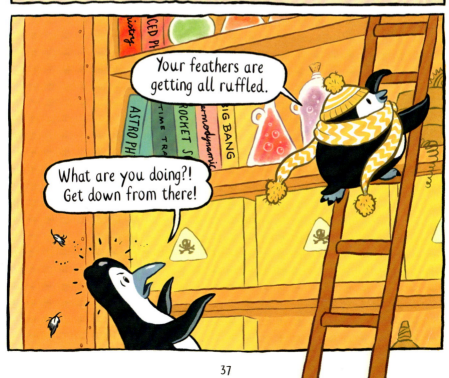

37

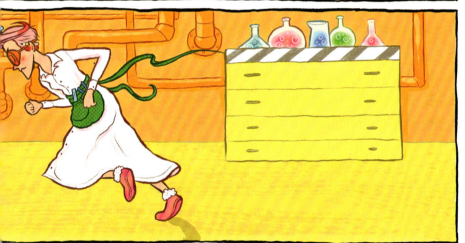

AAAGGGHHH!

49

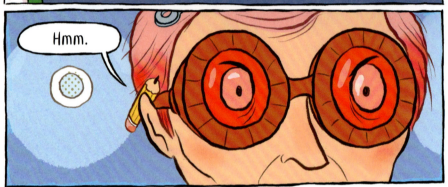

CHAPTER FOUR

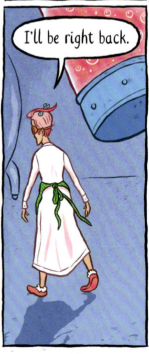

OVER THIS SIDE!

GO UP MY STEPS AND YOU CAN HIDE INSIDE.

I'm not sure about this!

Why not? It wants to help. It speaks Penguish.

I have a bad feeling.

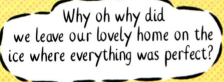

SOMEWHERE HOT!

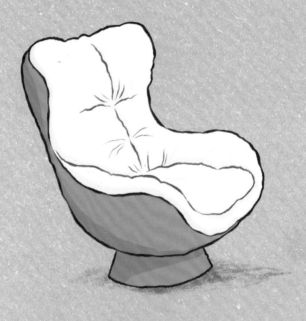

CHAPTER FIVE

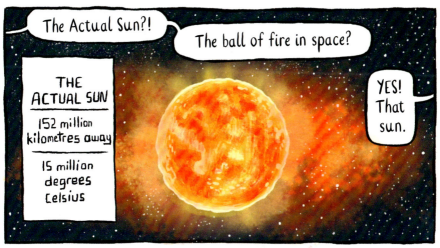

CHAPTER SIX

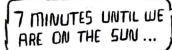

88

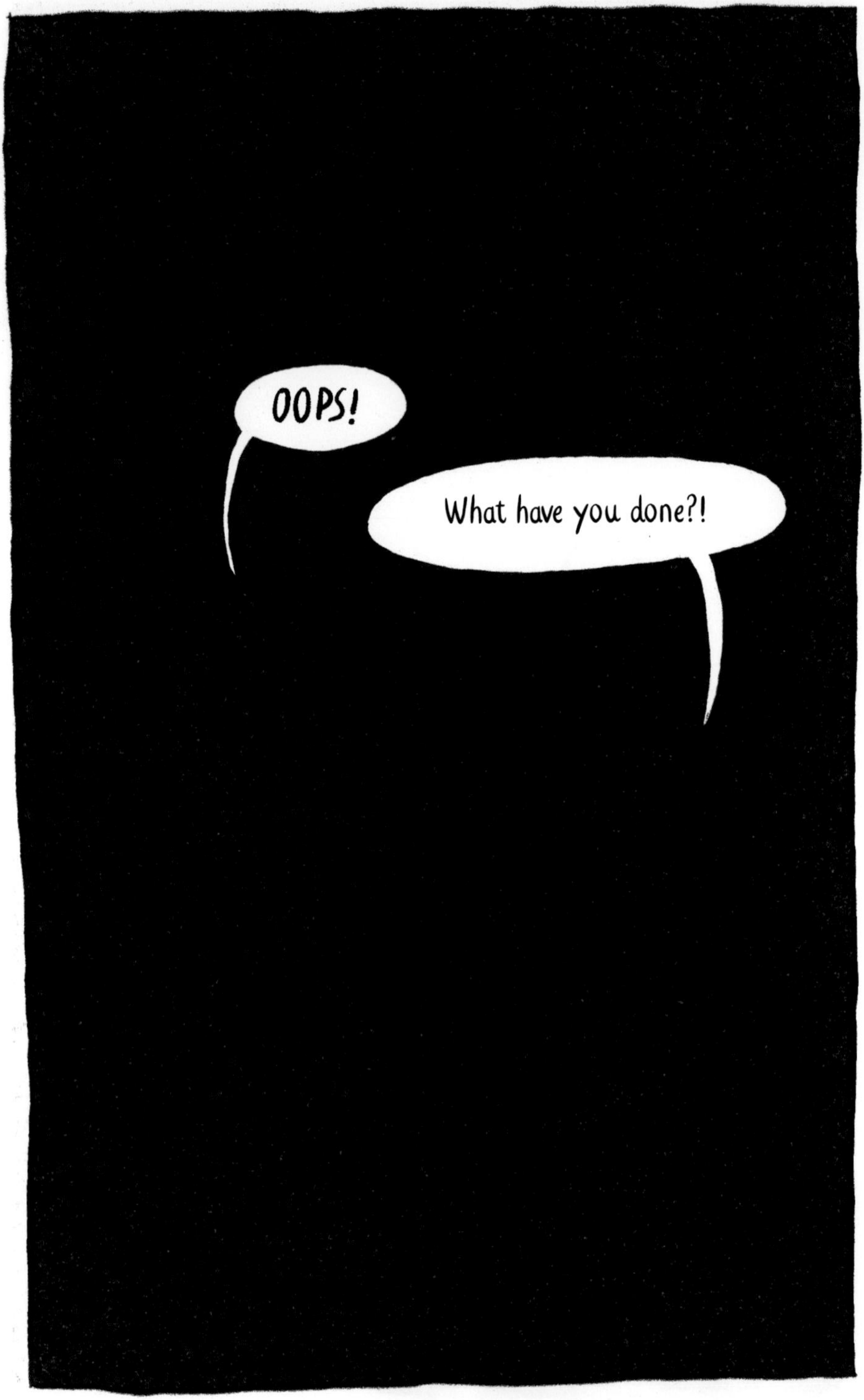
OOPS!
What have you done?!

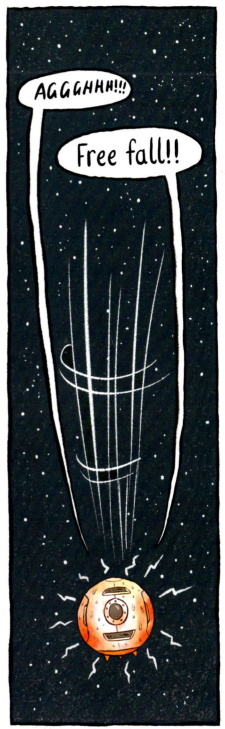

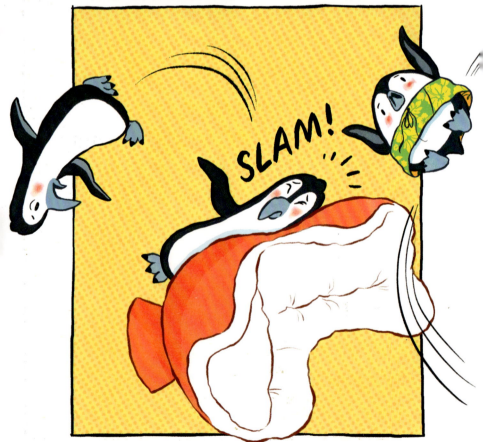

11 MINUTES UNTIL WE ARE ON EARTH.

Phew, I'm cooling down at last.

Me too.

You know, I think the kind robot might not be as kind as I thought.

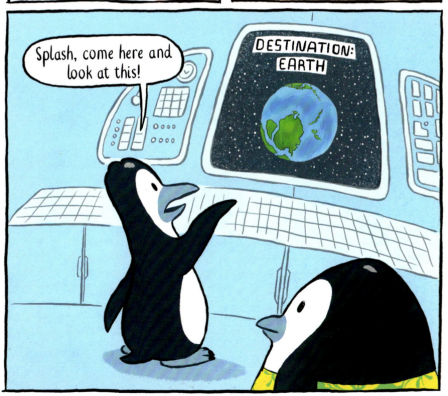

Squidgy, yes. But look, everything is totally green. No ice! Plus, Antarctica and Australia are joined togeth—

WE HAVE ARRIVED ON EARTH.

CHAPTER SEVEN

102

Pablo, we aren't going to catch our own food here! This is a luxury holiday!

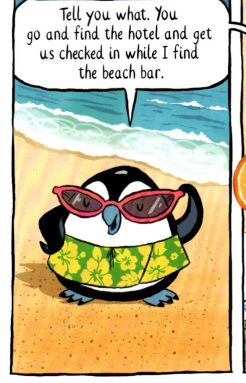

Tell you what. You go and find the hotel and get us checked in while I find the beach bar.

By the time you're back, I'll have us set up on a couple of sun loungers and we can order some snacks and mocktails.

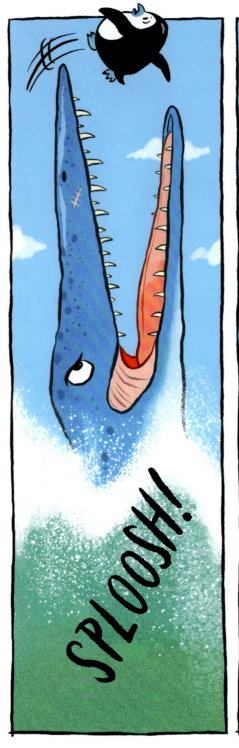

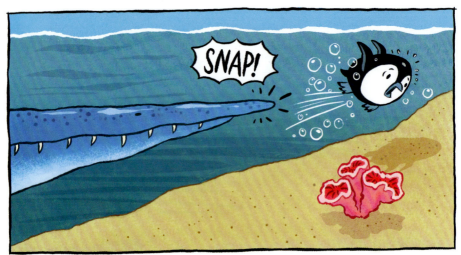

CHAPTER EIGHT

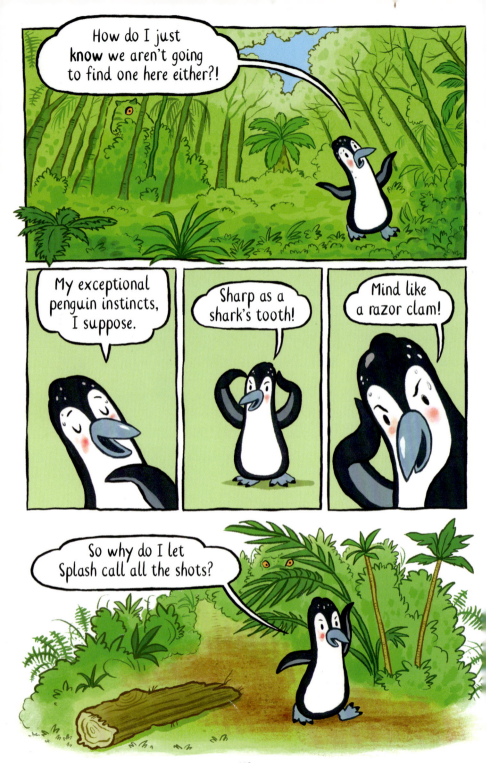

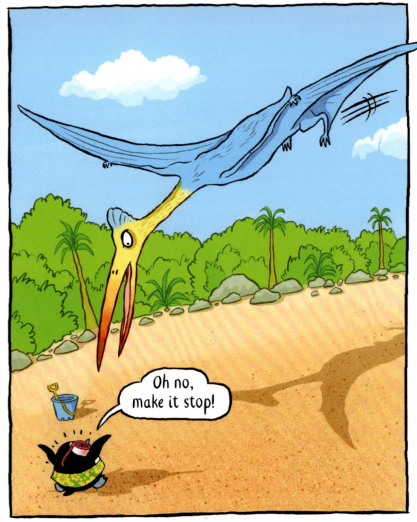

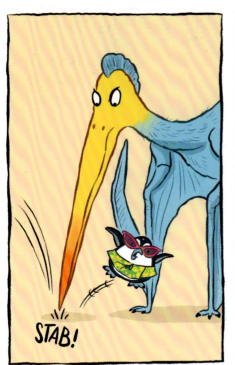

STAB!

STAB!

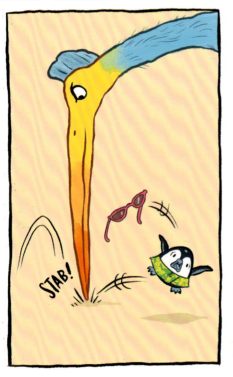

STAB!

YOINK!

CHAPTER NINE

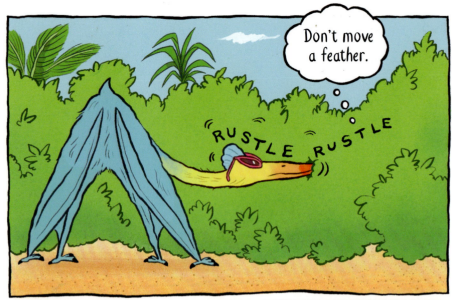

She's gone.

PHEW!

Now I must find Pablo.

I just hope he's having a better time on this HOLIDAY than I am.

CHAPTER TEN

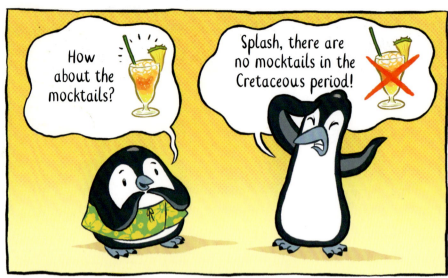

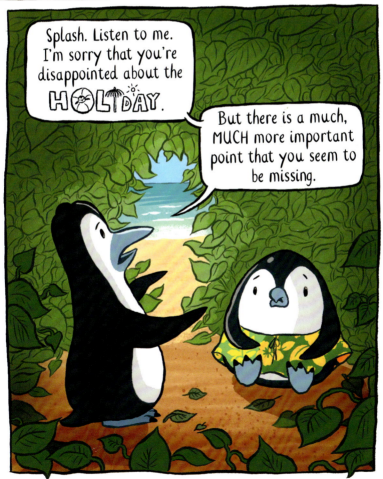

149

WE'RE SIXTY-FIVE MILLION YEARS AWAY FROM HOME AND OUR ONLY WAY TO GET BACK IS IN THE TIMEBENDER AND WHO KNOWS WHAT'S HAPPENED TO IT OUT THERE IN THE MEANTIME WITH ALL THESE CRAZY DINOSAURS CHARGING AROUND AND I'M HOT AND I'M HUNGRY AND ALL I WANT IS A KRILL POP AND TO EAT IT WHILE SITTING DOWN QUIETLY ON SOME COLD ICE!!!!

Can we please go home now?

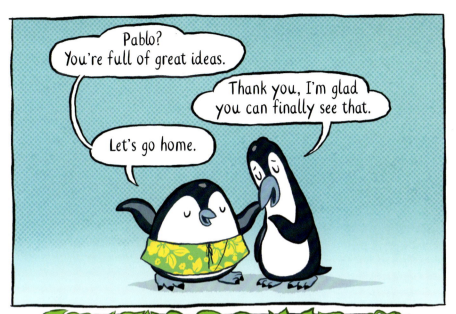

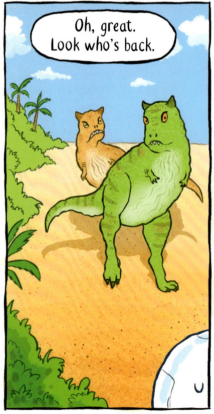

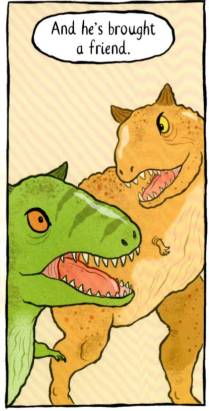

CHAPTER ELEVEN

We're **DOOMED.**

We're stuck here forever.

If we can't find another TimeBender, then we will have to fix the one we have!

How? Look at it!

Somehow! Some way! Sometime!

Actually, not 'sometime'.

It really has to happen NOW, before we bump into any more dinosaurs.

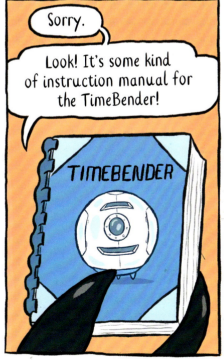

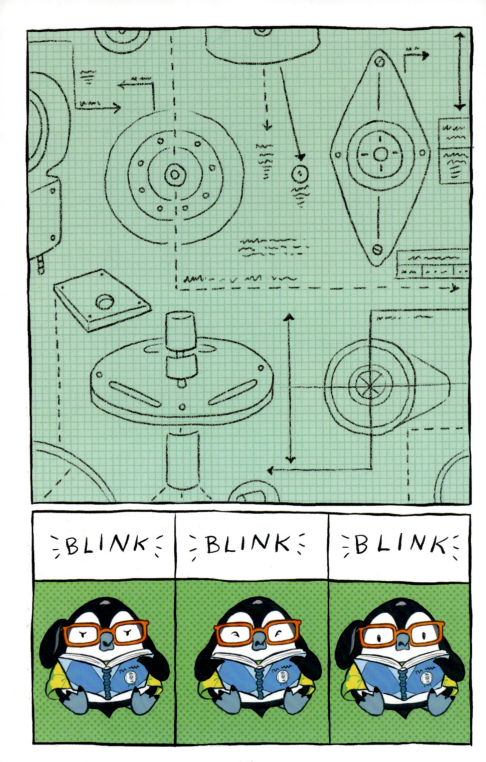

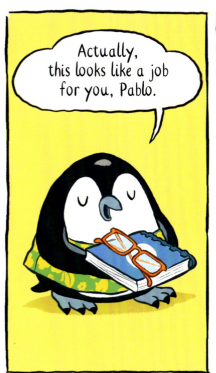

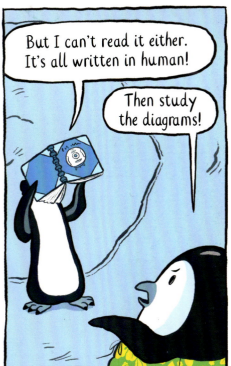

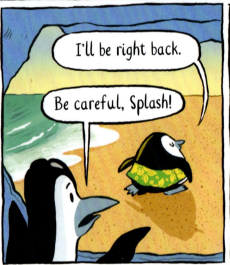

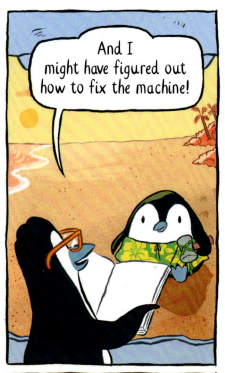

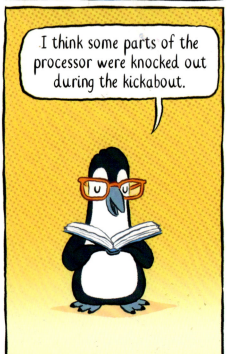

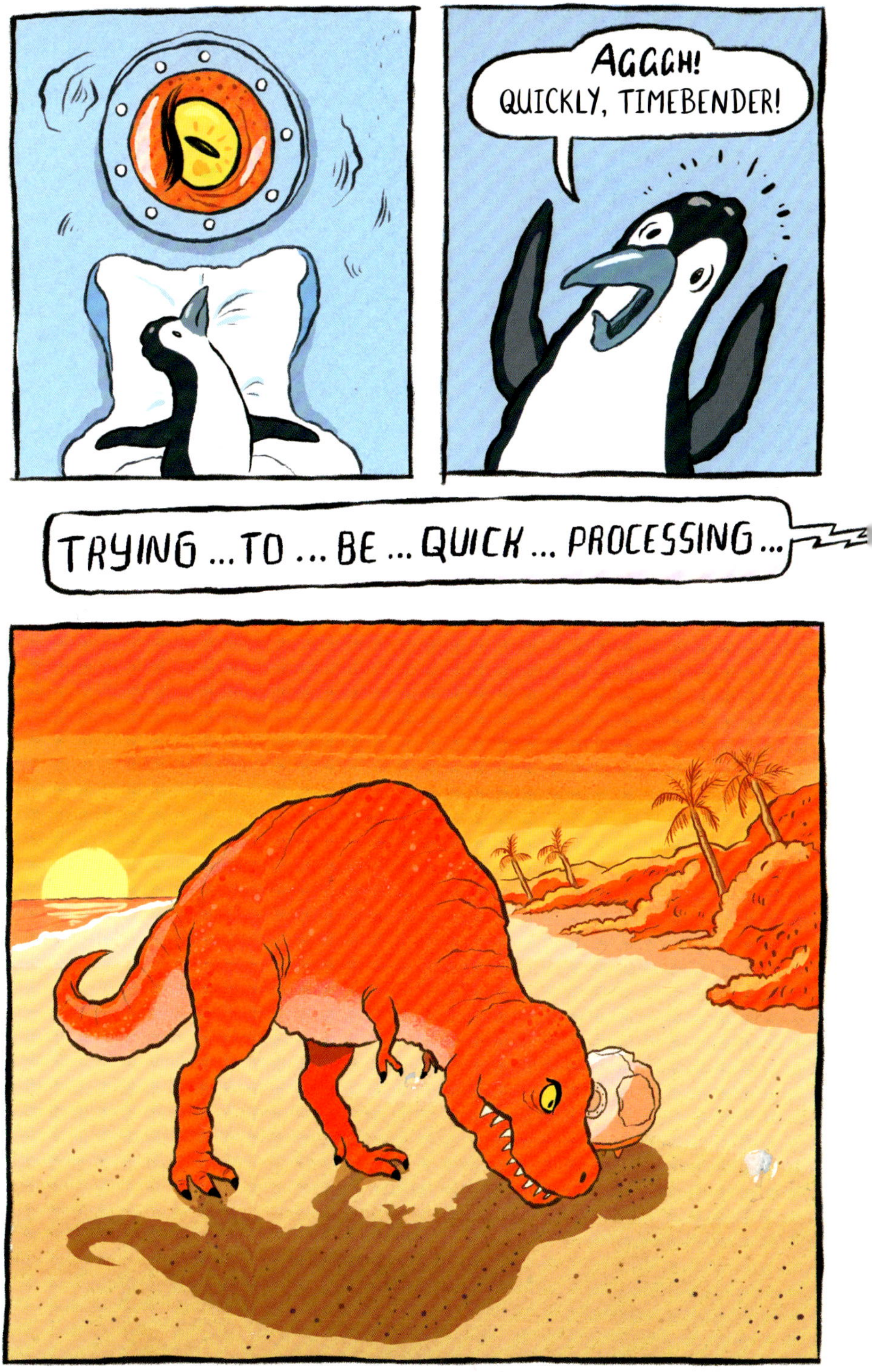
AGGGH!
QUICKLY, TIMEBENDER!
TRYING ... TO ... BE ... QUICK ... PROCESSING ...

CHAPTER TWELVE

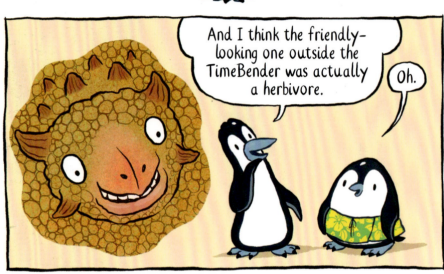

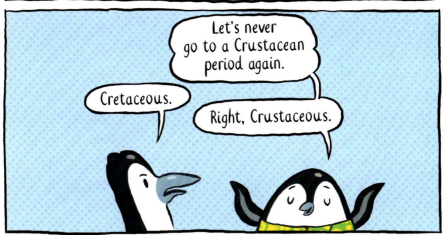

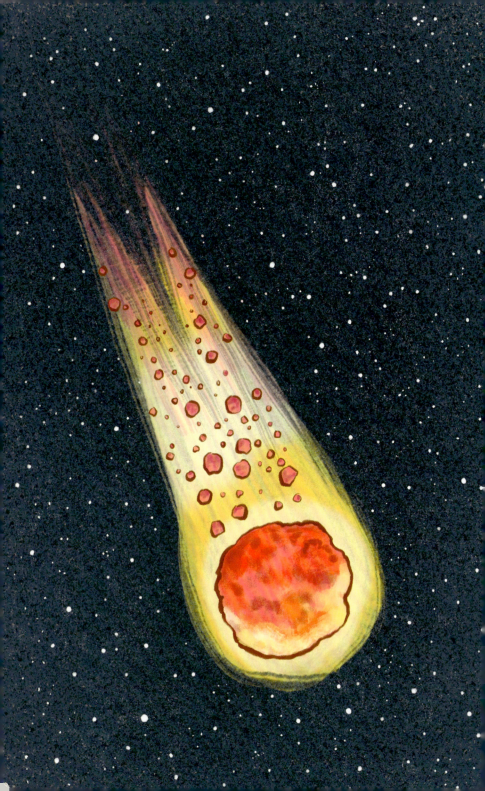

CHAPTER THIRTEEN

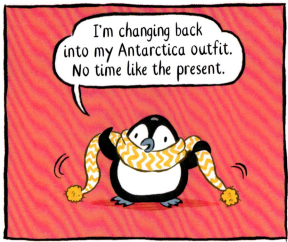

Behold my PTD — Penguish Translation Device.

It's my own invention, and once I put it on, we will understand each other perfectly.

CHAPTER FOURTEEN

Last one down the hill is a rotten squid!

THE END

MATCH THE SPEECH BUBBLES TO THE CHARACTERS

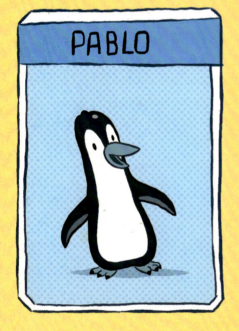

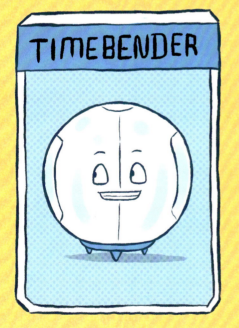

HOW TO DRAW PABLO

YAY!

1. Draw a pear shape.

2. Add some tufts.

3. Give him two dots for eyes, and a beak.

4. Give him feet and flippers for walking and talking.

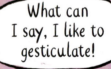

What can I say, I like to gesticulate!

5. Draw a line from his beak, round the edge of his body and back to his beak. The outer part can be filled in black. You can fill in his claws too.

HOW TO DRAW SPLASH

1. Draw an egg shape.

2. Start to add her hat and scarf details.

3. Her scarf has a zigzag pattern and bobbles at the end. Her hat has stripes. Add her feet.

4. Put her flippers on her hips to make her look impatient.

5. Give her two dots for eyes. Her beak is smaller than Pablo's. Draw a line around her body and face and fill in her claws.

FACTS

About 225 million years ago, all of Earth's continents were joined together in one big supercontinent called Pangaea.

PERMIAN

Roughly 200 million years ago, Pangaea started to break apart very, very, VERY slowly, over millions of years.

TRIASSIC

This is called continental drift. Look at how Earth appeared while Pablo and Splash were on their holiday in the Cretaceous period.

CRETACEOUS

The continents are still moving today, but we don't notice because it's happening so gradually.

PRESENT DAY

Ah, so THAT's why it looked all squidgy on the screen.

Tylosaurus was a predatory marine reptile that measured up to fourteen metres long. It was the deadliest hunter of the Cretaceous seas.

I can't believe you thought that was a whale, Splash.

Quetzalcoatlus was a flying reptile that lived during the Late Cretaceous period. It's the largest known flying animal to have ever existed. It towered at five metres high, about as tall as today's giraffe.

Hey, that's her! She's the one who stole my sunglasses!

Ankylosaurus was a herbivorous Cretaceous dinosaur. It moved very slowly, at about three miles per hour, but it was difficult for carnivores to attack because of its armour of horns and its club-shaped tail, which it used to fight off predators.

Ah, I was right.

Carnotaurus was a horned, carnivorous dinosaur that lived during the Late Cretaceous period. It had diminutive arms but a powerful tail and legs, and it weighed up to 2,100 kilograms.

I'm having an unpleasant flash-back!

Tyrannosaurus rex was a carnivorous dinosaur that lived during the Late Cretaceous period. It had a mouth full of teeth the size of penguin flippers and it measured up to twelve metres long and six metres tall.

Na-na-na-na-na, you can't catch us!

PABLO AND SPLASH'S COMPLETELY AND ABSOLUTELY TRUE FACTS

Krill pops are flippers down the most delicious snack ever.

FACT!

Penguish is the most beautifully complex language with millions of different sounds. It's very hard to learn, so don't feel bad if you don't know any.

The first ever game of **football** took place on a beach during the Cretaceous period 65 million years ago. The players were both Carnotaurus dinosaurs.

The **hammer** was invented during the Cretaceous period by Pablo and Splash rather than during the Stone Age, as previously thought.

That was just me, actually.

Dinosaurs might still roam the earth today if Pablo and Splash had warned them about the asteroid, which wiped them out just a few millennia after this story. (Good thing they didn't though, because then humans would never have evolved and you wouldn't be reading this book.)

HUDDLING

Penguins huddle together in tightly packed groups to conserve heat and to shelter from the fierce winds in the bitterly cold temperatures of Antarctica.

You see? Bitterly, BITTERLY cold!

Yes, but we penguins are BUILT for cold weather, Splash.

Except me, but then I suppose I am incredibly unique!

While outside temperatures in Antarctica reach as low as -80 °C, the temperatures in the centre of a penguin huddle can climb to 37 °C. A process of rotation means that no penguin is left on the cold outer edges of the huddle for long.

SOUTHERN LIGHTS

The southern lights (*aurora australis*) are a naturally occurring light display which can best be seen from Antarctica. Auroras paint the skies of both the Arctic *and* Antarctic Circles, but because there is more land in the Arctic Circle, e.g. Canada, Scandinavia and Russia, there are more places from which to observe the northern lights (*aurora borealis*). The Antarctic Circle is extremely remote, cold and inaccessible to humans and for this reason we don't hear as much about the southern lights, but they are just as impressive and beautiful.

Even more beautiful, I'd say.

Me too.

ABOUT THE AUTHOR

Sheena Dempsey is a children's book author and illustrator from Cork, Ireland. She has illustrated over thirty books for children but *Pablo and Splash* is her first graphic novel. She lives happily by the sea in Folkestone, Kent with her husband, Mick, and their perpetually hungry greyhound, Jeremy. In 2020, during the first lockdown, she produced a webcomic called Penguin Chronicles in which she and her husband appeared as penguins. Pablo and Splash are based on the characters from that webcomic.

Wait for me!

THANKS

No penguin is an island and I could not have made this book without the cheerleading or feedback of a much larger huddle of penguins. Sincere thanks to Maeve O'Connell for her excellent early thoughts. Thanks to my previous agent Felicity Trew for her feedback when this book idea was still very much in its egg. Huge thanks to my stellar agent Sallyanne Sweeney, who made what seemed impossible happen. Thanks to my critique group Claudia Boldt and Fabi Santiago for their incisive and honest feedback. Thanks to everyone at Bloomsbury, firstly commissioning editor Zöe Griffiths, who helped these penguins find their feet. Thanks to my new editor, Alex Antscherl, for her advice and for adopting these penguins as her own *and* for sending me such positive, encouraging tidbits of feedback. I can't thank my art director, Juliette Rechatin, enough, for her expert eye and for fielding so ... many ... emails. Thanks as ever to my family, Pat, Aoife and Darragh. Thanks to publishing pal Niamh Mulvey. Thanks to my niece Emily Dempsey for helping me draw the grains of sand on page 115! Thanks to physics professor Paul Tangney for answering my time-travel question. Thanks to all the supporters of my webcomic Penguin Chronicles — your response encouraged me to bring these penguins further. But the biggest thanks are for my husband, Mick: muse, sounding board and mate for life. This book is for him.

Let's go, Pablo, this is boring.